Clue Jr.™

The Case of the Stolen Jewel

Book created nter

Written by Michael Teitelbaum and Steve Morganstern

Illustrated by Sam Viviano

Based on characters from the Parker Brothers game

A Creative Media Applications Production

SCHOLASTIC INC.
New York Toronto London Auckland Sydney

ISBN 0-590-47908-3

12   8 9/9 0/0

Printed in the U.S.A.   40

First Scholastic printing, January 1995

Contents

Introduction

Meet the members of the Clue Club.

Samantha Scarlet, Peter Plum, Georgie Green, Wendy White, Mortimer Mustard, and Polly Peacock.

These young detectives are all in the same fourth-grade class. The thing they have most in common, though, is their love of mysteries. They formed the Clue Club to talk about mystery books they have read, mystery TV shows and movies they like to watch, and also, to play their favorite game, Clue Jr.

These mystery fans are pretty sharp when it comes to solving real-life mysteries, too. They all use their wit and deductive skills to crack the cases in this book.

1

You can match *your* wits with this gang of junior detectives to solve the eight mysteries. Can you guess who did it? Check the solution that appears upside down after the story to see if you were right!

The Case of the Big-Top Burglary

Every week the Clue Club has a meeting. This week the meeting was at Mortimer Mustard's house. All the members were sitting in Mortimer's den. They were waiting for Mortimer to check the mail.

"They're here! They're here!" Mortimer Mustard shouted as he raced from his mailbox back to the den.

"You got the tickets from your uncle?" asked Georgie Green.

"You bet!" exclaimed Mortimer. "We're all going to the circus!"

Mortimer Mustard's Uncle Fred was a clown in a world-famous circus. He had been promising for weeks to send Mortimer free tickets to the circus for all the members of the Clue Club.

"Not only that," continued Mortimer,

3

"but he's invited us to visit him in his trailer before the show!"

"Excellent," said Peter Plum. "A behind-the-scenes look at the magical world of the big top."

"I love the circus," said Samantha Scarlet. "I think the bareback-riding ladies are the best part. They're so beautiful."

"No way," said Georgie Green. "The coolest guy in the circus is the lion tamer. He sticks his head right into the lion's mouth."

"I like the high-wire walkers," said Wendy White. "They're so brave."

"My favorite are the trapeze artists," added Polly Peacock. "It's almost like they can fly!"

"Actually," began Peter, "the person I admire the most is the ringmaster. He has to keep all three rings of action moving along in an organized fashion. That's the circus job I would like."

"It's the clowns for me," said Mortimer. "But with one in the family, I guess I'm

4

prejudiced. Besides, he got us the free tickets!"

Everyone laughed and gave each other high fives. Excitement filled the room as the six friends talked about their upcoming visit to the circus.

Finally the big day came. The six Clue Club members arrived at the circus grounds one hour before show time. Hanging on the large big-top tent was a huge poster announcing the various circus acts.

"Look!" shouted Mortimer. "Uncle Fred's picture is the biggest one, and it's right in the middle of the poster."

The others all gazed at the colorful poster.

"There's Rinaldo, the Singing Ringmaster," Peter pointed out.

" 'Lovely Linda and her Lady Lions,' " read Samantha. "Sounds wonderful."

"This guy looks cool," said Georgie, pointing to a picture of Blasto the Human Cannonball.

"Let's go meet Uncle Fred," said Mortimer, leading the others. "He said he's in trailer number nine."

The others followed him until they came to trailer number nine. Mortimer knocked on the door, but got no answer.

"That's strange," commented Mortimer. "He knew we were coming. I wonder where he could be."

A few seconds later, Uncle Fred came running up to his trailer, huffing and puffing. He was all out of breath.

"Uncle Fred!" shouted Mortimer. "Are you all right? Where have you been?"

"I'm okay, Mortimer," replied Uncle Fred. "I'm sorry I'm late. But the strangest thing just happened. About half an hour ago I found a note on my trailer from Lovely Linda. She asked me to meet her all the way on the other side of the circus grounds. She said it was urgent."

"What happened?" asked Mortimer.

"Well, when I got there, I searched the whole area but I couldn't find Linda anywhere," explained Uncle Fred. "I guess it was just some kind of dumb prank. . . . Anyway, come on into my trailer."

Mortimer and his friends followed Uncle Fred into the trailer. "Now," said Uncle Fred, "what can I tell you about the circus?"

"Tell me about Lovely Linda and her Lady Lions," asked Samantha.

"Linda is one of my best friends here at the circus," said Uncle Fred. "That's why I was so concerned when I got her note. Wait until you see her act. She's one of the best lion tamers I've ever worked with."

"Does Rinaldo really sing?" asked Peter.

"Oh, yes," replied Uncle Fred. "He used to sing with the opera. But he gave it up to join the circus."

"Wow!" said Wendy. "How romantic!"

"How about Blasto the Human Cannonball?" asked Georgie. "He sounds really cool."

At the mention of Blasto's name, Uncle

Fred scowled. "That creep is just a crazy egomaniac," said Uncle Fred angrily. "Ever since the circus poster came out when we started this tour a year ago, he's been mad at me. He's upset that my picture is the big one in the center and his is smaller and on the side. It wasn't my decision to do that. And besides, I've been with the circus longer."

"He doesn't sound like a very nice guy," said Polly.

"He isn't," replied Uncle Fred. "It's like he's declared war on me. After almost a year on the road together, we just can't stand each other."

BOOM! BOOM! BOOM! A loud knocking came at the door.

"Who can that be?" wondered Uncle Fred. When he opened the door, two police officers were standing there.

"Excuse me," began one of the officers. "Sorry to bother you, but a large sum of money was stolen from the circus office

8

within the last half hour. We're searching everyone's quarters. Just routine, you know."

"Of course," said Uncle Fred. "Come in."

The police searched every corner of Uncle Fred's trailer. They were about to leave when one of the officers shouted out, "What have we here?"

The officer had been going through a chest of drawers. Among the clown wigs that Uncle Fred kept in one of the drawers, the officer found a fat wad of one hundred dollar bills.

"Can you explain this, Mr. Mustard?" asked the officer.

"I don't understand how that money got there," said Uncle Fred. "I haven't been in my trailer for the past half hour. I was on the other side of the circus grounds, searching for Linda."

"Can you prove this, Mr. Mustard?" asked the officer.

"Yes," cried Uncle Fred. "I can. I have

a note from Linda asking me to meet her. It's right here on my trunk."

Uncle Fred turned around and looked at the top of his trunk.

"The note!" he exclaimed. "It's gone!"

"I'm sorry, Mr. Mustard," said the officer, "but you'll have to come with us."

The police officer slapped handcuffs on Uncle Fred and led him out the trailer door. When he stepped outside, Blasto the Human Cannonball was waiting.

"Thought you could get away with a little funny business, eh Freddy!" Blasto taunted him. "Well I guess I get the last laugh!"

"Oh, blow it out your ears, powder puff," retorted Fred. "If I didn't have these cuffs on I'd give you such a shot!"

Never one to let Fred get the last word, Blasto fired back. "Money in your wig drawer?" he quipped. "You can't *wig*gle out of this one! You're out of here! Har har har!"

Suddenly Mortimer Mustard raced up to

the police officer. "My uncle didn't do it!" he cried. "I'm positive!"

How did Mortimer know his uncle was innocent? And who *did* take the money?

Solution
The Case of the Big-Top Burglary

"My uncle didn't take the money," said Mortimer. "Blasto took the money and put it here to get Uncle Fred in trouble!"

"Why, that kid is nuts!" shouted Blasto. "He doesn't know what he's talking about."

"Uncle Fred told us about the fight that he and Blasto have been having for the past year," continued Mortimer. "It looks like Blasto couldn't resist getting the last insult. The only problem is, he wasn't here when the trailer was searched, and nobody had said a word about where we found the money. Blasto couldn't have known it was hidden in the wig drawer unless he had planted it there himself! Blasto lost his cool arguing with Uncle Fred and couldn't resist making the bad wig joke. I'll bet he even took Linda's note, as well."

Sure enough, when the police searched Blasto's pockets, they found the note. Blasto had actually written it himself, then removed it while putting the money in the wig drawer.

"Looks like the joke's on you, Blasto," said Uncle Fred with a grin, as the police led the true criminal away. "A human cannonball should know better than to shoot his mouth off!"

Uncle Fred finally had the last word.

2

The Case of the Headless Snowman

Peter Plum leaped from his bed and dashed to his bedroom window. It was bright and early Saturday morning, and it had finally stopped snowing.

There had been a big storm Friday afternoon, and it continued all night long. But now the sun was shining and there was at least ten inches of snow on the ground in Peter's front yard. He ran downstairs and found his mother in the kitchen with the family dog, Bizzy.

"Mom!" said Peter. "May I go out and play in the snow?"

"First you need to have a nice warm breakfast. Then you may go out. I have to take Bizzy to the V-E-T for his booster shots and drop off this bag of clothes at the Salvation Army downtown." Peter's mother spelled out the word *vet* because it was a word that Bizzy knew. He hated to go to the vet, and would hide whenever he heard that word. Spelling out the word helped, but even then Bizzy sometimes seemed to "guess" he was about to go. The Plums had to be very tricky.

After his mother left, Peter made himself a bowl of instant oatmeal. He gobbled it up as fast as he could. Then Peter put on his big boots and his ski jacket and ran outdoors.

"This is the best!" he shouted out loud, reaching into the snow to make his first snowball of the year. "Hey, this snow is perfect for packing. I'm going to make a snowman."

Peter put his snowball on the ground and rolled it over and over in the snow. Soon he had to push with both hands. After he had made a good-sized mound, he made another ball — a little bit smaller — and lifted it up onto the first mound.

"Now to make his head," Peter said,

bending down to scoop up another handful of snow. In a few minutes, the snowman was complete. Peter stood back to admire his work.

"All I need now are some finishing touches," he said.

Peter went back into the house and returned with an armful of things for the snowman — a floppy old hat, some buttons to make the snowman's eyes and mouth, a carrot for his nose, and a scarf. Peter tied the long red-and-white scarf around the snowman's neck.

"There!" he said. "I have to admit, you are the best snowman I've ever built. I've got to get a picture before you start to melt."

Peter ran inside to get his camera — but unfortunately, he was out of film. "Rats!" he exclaimed. Then he had an idea. He went to the phone and punched in the number of his friend and fellow Clue Club member Mortimer Mustard. Mortimer, he knew, also had a camera.

Mortimer answered the phone on the first ring.

"Hi, Mortimer," Peter said. "Isn't this snow great?"

"Yeah, I can hardly wait to get outdoors," Mortimer said. "My mom is making me eat a nice warm breakfast first."

"Well, hurry up and come over," Peter told him. "Do you have any film in your camera?"

"Sure," his friend said. "Why?"

"I need a picture of the great snowman I just made," Peter explained. "I was wondering if — "

Just then Peter heard a sharp cry coming from the front yard. "Hold on a minute, Mortimer," he said, putting down the phone. He ran to the front door, opened it, and looked outside.

Again he heard the sharp cry. He caught a glimpse of a blonde-haired girl running away from the house.

I wonder what that was all about? Peter thought. He looked around the yard — and that's when he saw it. His snowman was headless! Someone had knocked the head off the body, and it was lying smashed on the ground. Not only that, but the snowman's red-and-white scarf was gone.

Peter raced back to the phone. "Mortimer," he said, "you've got to get over here fast. We've got a snowman smasher to catch."

In no time at all Mortimer arrived at Peter's house. "What happened? he asked, looking at the snowman. "Do you know who did it? Are there any clues?"

"Well," Peter began, "I heard a scream, then I saw a blonde-haired girl running away."

"A blonde-haired girl?" repeated Mortimer. ". . . Um, our friend Wendy has blonde hair, and she doesn't live too far from you."

Peter and Mortimer went inside. "I think I'll give Wendy a call," said Peter.

"I was just about to call *you*," Wendy White said when she heard Peter's voice.

"I was coming over to see you this morning with my parrot. I wanted to show you the neat trick I just taught Petunia. But when I got near your house, your dog Bizzy saw Petunia and started chasing me, trying to get at her. I ran away and Bizzy chased me halfway home!"

"Nice story, Wendy," said Peter. "But it can't be true. My mom took Bizzy to the vet this morning."

"What?" exclaimed Wendy.

"I think you'd better come over so we can talk about this," Peter said.

Wendy rushed over to Peter's house. The three friends stood over the wrecked snowman.

"Your dog chased my bird! I swear it," Wendy said.

"Impossible!" Peter said. "You wrecked my snowman!"

"Wait a minute," said Mortimer. "I've heard what Peter thinks happened, but I'd like to hear Wendy's side of the story myself."

Wendy repeated what she had said on the phone to Peter. Mortimer started walking around the snowman, looking carefully on the ground. Suddenly, he stopped.

"Don't anyone move," he said. "I believe Wendy is telling the truth. She didn't destroy the snowman."

Who did wreck the snowman, and how did Mortimer know Wendy was telling the truth?

Solution
The Case of the Headless Snowman

"Look very carefully at the tracks in the snow, Peter," Mortimer told him. "You can see our tracks, and you can see where Wendy ran across the yard. But there are other tracks there, too — smaller ones."

"You're right, Mortimer!" Peter exclaimed. "And they look just like a dog's paw prints. But how could . . . ?"

Just then, Peter's mother pulled into the driveway. She looked upset as she got out of the car.

"Oh, Peter!" she called. "Have you seen Bizzy anywhere? I got all the way to the vet's and found he wasn't in the backseat! He must have jumped out and hidden when I loaded the bag of clothes for the Salvation Army in the front."

"No, Mom, I haven't seen him," Peter said, "but don't worry. I have a feeling he's around here somewhere."

The three kids searched the yard. The

paw prints lead them straight to the open garage. And there, curled up on the red-and-white scarf, lay one sleepy puppy.

"Bad dog," Peter scolded. "I'm sorry I didn't believe you, Wendy."

"That's okay," Wendy told him. "How could you know? Looks like Bizzy played a pretty good trick on us."

"But he's not going to get out of a trip to the V-E-T," Peter's mother said.

They all laughed.

"Speaking of tricks . . ," Wendy said, "you've got to see Petunia do a flip on her swing."

And so the three members of the Clue Club adjourned to Wendy's house for hot chocolate and a parrot performance — but not before they had put the snowman back together again, scarf and all.

3

The Case of the Rotten Rally

The Clue Club had gathered at Georgie Green's house for a few rounds of Clue Jr.

"All right!" exclaimed Georgie, as the game ended. "My team wins again."

"You just got lucky today, Georgie," said Polly Peacock, captain of the losing team. "Next time it will be different."

"Oh, my!" said Peter Plum, standing up quickly. "Look at the time. We've almost missed the beginning of the local news."

The other kids sighed and rolled their eyes.

"Georgie, may I turn on your television to watch the news?" asked Peter.

"Sure," replied Georgie. "I'm in such a good mood from winning that I'm up for anything."

The others all followed Peter into the

25

living room, where he flipped on the TV. Everyone got comfortable and settled in to watch the news.

After a few stories about local politics, upcoming community meetings, and a look at the weather, the newscaster said something that grabbed everyone's interest.

"Well, this Sunday, out at Stewart Stadium, there's going to be quite an event," she began. "The biggest Monster Truck Rally in the U.S. is coming to town. Here's some more about it."

All six Clue Club members sat up straight.

"Wow!" exclaimed Mortimer Mustard. "Monster Trucks are about the coolest things in the world!"

"Shhh, quiet," said Wendy White. "Here it comes!"

The image of a huge truck with gigantic tires rolling over four cars filled the TV screen. The announcer yelled at the top of his lungs.

"Sunday! Sunday! Sunday!" he screamed, as the truck climbed a steep hill made from the bodies of crushed cars. "For one day only at Stewart Stadium, it's TRUCK-MANIA! Don't miss the United States' biggest Monster Truck Rally ever. See Daredevil Dan and his Terrible Truck of Doom, Hairpin Harry and his Tremendous Truck of Terror, and Big Bertha and her Vanquishing Van. All this Sunday at Stewart Stadium. Tickets on sale today. Miss it, and regret it for the rest of your lives!"

The Clue Club members fell back in their seats in silence. The local news resumed, but no one was listening. Not even Peter.

"Awesome!" exclaimed Samantha Scarlet, summing up everyone's feelings. "This is going to be the greatest Monster Truck Rally ever!"

"And Stewart Stadium is a really cool place," added Wendy. "You know they recently added a dome so that events can be held in any kind of weather."

"We've got to get tickets to this," said Mortimer.

"How are we going to do that?" asked Polly. "First we have to get to the stadium to buy the tickets, then we'd need another ride on the day of the rally."

"No problem," chimed in Peter. "My dad can drive us. Our new minivan may not be a Monster Truck, but it will certainly hold all of us."

"Good idea, Peter," said Georgie. "I'm going to go get my allowance money for a ticket. You call your dad."

Peter raced to the phone and quickly called his dad. Mr. Plum not only agreed to drive them to the rally on Sunday, but he told Peter that he would drive over right then and pick them up so that they could buy the tickets.

Peter's dad arrived in his minivan a short while later. The Clue Club kids were all waiting in front of Georgie's house.

"Thanks, Mr. Plum," said each club member as they scrambled into the van.

"Oh, you're more than welcome," replied Mr. Plum. "You know, the week after the rally they're holding a rock and mineral exhibition at the town armory. We could swing by there and pick up tickets to that as well!"

"That sounds neat, Dad!" said Peter enthusiastically.

The others all smiled politely.

"Thanks, Mr. Plum," said Mortimer. "But I think we only have enough money for the rally."

"Well, then, what are we waiting for?" asked Mr. Plum. "Let's go get those tickets!"

Mr. Plum drove each of the friends home so that they could pick up their allowance money. He then drove them out to Stewart Stadium.

The Clue Club kids hurried from the van. The stadium's large silver dome was gleaming from the afternoon sun. "What a great day!" Wendy said as they ran up to the box office.

Peter collected everyone's money and stepped up to the window. "I'd like to purchase six tickets to Truck-Mania, please."

"Sorry, kid," said the box office clerk. "All sold out."

"What!" exclaimed Georgie. "But the TV said that the tickets went on sale today!"

"That's right, kid," said the clerk. "I've never seen anything like it. The rally sold out within one hour of the tickets going on sale."

The six friends returned to the van.

"Now we're going to miss the best show ever," moaned Mortimer.

"Not necessarily," said Georgie.

"What do you mean?" asked Samantha, as all the kids listened intently.

"I know how we can get tickets," said Georgie. "I have a cousin who has a girl-friend whose brother works for a guy who knows someone who works at the stadium. He can get tickets to any show! The only problem is that they're going to cost a lot more."

The kids thought it over and all decided that it was worth digging deep into their pockets for this most awesome of events.

Mr. Plum dropped the kids back at Georgie's house, where they all thanked him. Georgie dashed to the phone and called his cousin Grant.

Half an hour later, Grant arrived with six tickets to Truck-Mania.

"This is going to cost you little squirts," said Grant. "Double the regular price."

"We know," said Peter. "But for this rally we think it's worth it."

"All right," said Grant, reaching into his pocket. "Now where's the dough?"

Each of the Clue Club members handed over his or her money to Grant. Peter took the six tickets and examined them carefully. He began to read aloud.

"Admit One to Truck-Mania, Sunday,

May 8, Stewart Stadium. Section 120, Row C, Seat 7. In case of rain, rally will be held on Sunday, May 15."

"Wow," said Georgie. "We're going to get to see the rally after all."

"Just a moment, Grant," said Peter, as Grant headed for the door. "These tickets are fakes. We want our money back!"

How did Peter know that the tickets were fakes?

Solution
The Case of the Rotten Rally

"What do you mean, 'fake'?" shouted Grant.

"Look right here," said Peter, pointing to the bottom of one of the tickets. "It says 'In case of rain, rally will be held on Sunday May 15.' But Stewart Stadium has a domed roof. Therefore they never have rain dates. These tickets are clearly phoney."

Grant groaned. Faced with the truth, he gave the kids back their money and left.

"At least we got our money back," said Wendy.

"Yes, but now we're not going to get to see the rally," said Mortimer.

"Well," said Peter, "we can always go to the rock and mineral exhibition with my dad."

The others all groaned as they went back to set up Clue Jr. for another game.

4

The Case of the
Thanksgiving Turkey

Though it was early November, the students in Ms. Redding's fourth-grade class were already thinking about Thanksgiving. All the members of the Clue Club were in Ms. Redding's class and they were beginning to get into the holiday spirit.

"I love Thanksgiving," said Samantha Scarlet. "The food, the family, the big parade. It's one of my favorite holidays."

"I like it best because I know that Christmas is only a month away!" said Polly Peacock.

"I like eating turkey and watching football," said Georgie Green.

"I like recalling the first Thanksgiving," said Peter Plum. "Thinking about the Pilgrims and the Native Americans sitting down at the same table, sharing turkey and corn."

"Well, it's very interesting that you should mention that, Peter," said Ms. Redding. "Because that leads us to our special Thanksgiving project."

"Nice going, Peter," whispered Mortimer Mustard. "Now we've got to do a project."

"Class, please open your assignment books and listen very carefully," Ms. Redding continued. "I want you to carefully take notes."

The students in Ms. Redding's class opened their assignment notebooks and sat ready to write.

"You are each going to write and illustrate a Thanksgiving story," the teacher began.

"How exciting," said Peter.

"In your own words and your own pictures," Ms. Redding explained, "I want you to tell the story of that first Thanksgiving. The story of the Pilgrims and the

Native Americans. I want you to pay close attention to what they wore, what they ate, what the Pilgrims' ship looked like, and what the Native Americans' village looked like. All of this information can be found in books in the library."

Moans and groans broke out around the classroom. Suddenly Thanksgiving was not quite as popular as it had been a few minutes earlier.

Ms. Redding went on. "I'd like at least ten pictures from each of you, colored in, to go along with your story. They've got to be neatly drawn, and the assignment has got to be handed in on time. Write down the due date, November twelfth."

The students scribbled furiously in their notebooks and whispered to each other. When all the writing and murmuring ended, Ms. Redding went on with the day's lessons.

The bell sounded at three o'clock. As the students filed from the classroom, the Clue Club members gathered in the school yard to talk about their latest assignment.

"How are we going to do ten pictures and a story by November twelfth?" asked Samantha.

"It shouldn't be too tough, Samantha," replied Peter. "A couple of days in the reference section of the library, and you'll have all the information you need!"

Samantha just sighed, and the friends each headed home.

Over the next few weeks the students in Ms. Redding's class did their research, wrote their stories, and drew their pictures. Some, like Peter, used colored pencils and watercolors. Most, however, used crayons and markers. All agreed, it was one of the toughest, but most interesting, projects they had ever worked on.

Finally the big day arrived — November 12, the day the project was due.

One by one the students filed into Ms. Redding's classroom. Each one placed his or her project proudly on the teacher's desk. Everyone except Samantha Scarlet.

Samantha shuffled into the classroom nervously, tears streaming down her cheeks.

"Why, Samantha, what's the matter?" asked Ms. Redding.

"I can't believe it," Samantha wailed. "I worked for weeks on that project. I went to the library, did my research, wrote my story, drew my pictures, colored them in, and now for *this* to happen on the day it's due!"

"Just calm down and tell me what happened," said Ms. Redding.

Samantha pulled a big book from her backpack. "I took this book about Thanksgiving out of the library. I used it for my research. This morning I stuck my project into the book to protect it on my way to school. But now it's gone. It must have dropped out on the bus, or on my way to the bus stop, or, I don't know, it could have fallen anywhere."

"Are you sure it isn't in your backpack, or in another book?" asked the teacher.

"Nooo!" moaned Samantha. "I know exactly where I put it — between pages eleven and twelve of this big Thanksgiving book. I knew I'd remember it because the due date was eleven-twelve — November twelfth. That way I'd make extra sure that I'd know where it was. But now it's gone!"

Just then, Georgie Green spoke up. "Ms. Redding! Samantha is telling a lie! I'll bet she just never finished her assignment at all!"

Why does Georgie think that Samantha is lying?

Solution
The Case of the Thanksgiving Turkey

"Now, Georgie," began Ms. Redding. "It's not nice to accuse someone of lying. What proof do you have?"

"Samantha couldn't have stuck her project between pages eleven and twelve of that book," Georgie explained, "because page eleven is a right-hand page and page twelve is the back of the same page. There's no place between pages eleven and twelve to stick anything.

"I'm sorry, Samantha," continued Georgie, "but it looks like you're the Thanksgiving turkey in this class!"

"That's enough, Georgie," said Ms. Redding. "Samantha, because you lied and didn't do your project, I'm giving you a special assignment. In addition to doing the Thanksgiving project, you are to write a thousand word essay on why it is wrong to lie!"

The Case of the Mind Reader

The weekly meeting of the Clue Club was almost over. Three rounds of Clue Jr. had been played, and the kids were getting ready to go home. "If you could read my mind right now," said Mortimer Mustard, "what do you think you would see?"

"A very tiny object," quipped Georgie Green.

Everyone broke up laughing.

"Very funny, Georgie," said Mortimer. "But I meant that if you could read my mind, you'd know that I'd love to stop for some ice cream on the way home."

"Well, *I* believe in mind reading and ESP," said Peter Plum.

"Yeah, *e*xtra *s*cience *p*rojects, right, Peter?" said Polly Peacock.

"Very clever, Polly, but no," began

Peter. "ESP as in *extra* *s*ensory *p*erception. Mind reading, psychic phenomena, and other mysteries of the great unknown that is the human mind."

"The only unknown about *your* mind, Peter, is how you cram so many big words into such a tiny space," said Georgie.

"I think Peter's right," said Wendy White. "I believe that there are some things that just can't be explained by normal science."

"Maybe Georgie is right. Maybe there's no such thing as ESP," said Samantha Scarlet.

"Don't listen to Georgie, Samantha," said Wendy, her best friend in the Clue Club. "Georgie is just too small-minded to believe in higher concepts like ESP and mind reading."

"Well my mind is telling me that it's time to get out of here," said Mortimer. "I'm going home, but first, who wants to stop for ice cream?"

Everyone did.

* * *

The next day at school, when the bell for lunch sounded, the ESP and mind-reading discussion continued, as the members of the Clue Club filed from their classroom and walked together to the school cafeteria.

"I have ESP," said Georgie. "I'll bet I know what Mortimer brought for lunch — a bologna sandwich with lots of mustard and a banana."

"Nice try, Georgie," said Peter. "But we all know that Mortimer brings the same thing for lunch every day! I, myself, brought a grape jelly sandwich and a bright purple plum."

The friends settled in at their usual lunchroom table. When Mortimer opened his lunch box he got quite a shock.

"Oh, no," he said. "Here's my bologna sandwich with lots of mustard, but my mom forgot to give me dessert. No banana. This is terrible. You all know how much I love dessert. Does anybody want to trade

45

me their dessert for this sandwich?"

"I do like bologna sandwiches," said Wendy, "but not enough to give up my yummy slice of cake."

Nobody else was willing to trade with Mortimer.

Mortimer thought for a second. Then a sly smile crept over his face.

"You'll all be sorry when I become a famous mind reader," Mortimer Mustard said. "Why, I'll be rich and famous, on TV and everything, and you'll all be dying to visit me, but I won't have anything to do with you guys because you wouldn't share your desserts with me."

"Are you starting with that mind-reading stuff again," whined Georgie. "I keep telling you guys that that stuff is all phoney."

"Tell you what, Georgie," said Mortimer. "I'll read your mind. If I get it wrong, you get my delicious bologna sandwich. But if I'm right, I get your lime Jell-O."

"You got a deal, pal," said Georgie ea-

gerly. "What do I have to do?"

"Okay," said Mortimer. "Polly. Will you help us out?"

"Sure," said Polly.

"Georgie, I'm going to lead you through a mind-reading exercise, step by step," explained Mortimer. "I want you to whisper your answer at each step to Polly, so she knows that this is for real. Okay, here we go.

"First, Georgie, I want you to think of a number — any number at all. Got one? Good. Now whisper it to Polly."

"I picked *45*," Georgie whispered to Polly.

"Now, add the next highest number to the number you came up with," continued Mortimer. "For example, if you picked 10, add 11 to 10."

"I picked 45, so the next highest number would be 46. And 45 plus 46 equals *91*," whispered Georgie.

"Okay? Now add 9."

"If I add 9 to 91, I get *100*," whispered Georgie.

"Got that? Fine. Now divide that number in half."

"Okay, 100 divided in half equals *50*," whispered Georgie.

"And finally, subtract your original number from the result."

"If I take 45 away from 50, it equals *5*," whispered Georgie.

"Now, I want you to think very hard about the number you've come up with," said Mortimer, squeezing his forehead in heavy concentration. "Remember, you started with any number in the world, right? And now I'm going to read your mind and tell you what number you've come up with. Okay . . . I'm getting a vision. . . . Ooooooh, it's coming in clearer now. . . . You're thinking of . . . the number *5*! Am I right?"

A baffled Georgie looked at Mortimer with a stunned expression. He handed over his Jell-O to Mortimer, who gleefully began to gobble it up.

"I guess you really *can* read minds," said Georgie.

"Only enough to know that your mind is too dumb to realize you've been fooled!" said Peter. "It's a trick. And I know how it's done!"

Do you know how the trick was done?

Solution
The Case of the Mind Reader

The others all listened intently as Peter explained:

"No matter what number you start out with, the result will always be 5!

"Let's say you choose 15 to start. The next highest number is 16, and 15 plus 16 equals 31. Now add 9 and get 40. Divide the result in half and get 20, then subtract 15 and get 5!

"Let's look closely at the way this works:

"Take your original number: 15.

"The next higher number is really 15 plus 1.

"Add them up and you get 15 plus 15 plus 1.

"Add another 9 and you get 15 plus 15 plus 10.

"Now divide it by 2 — that's the same as subtracting the 15 you added in the second step, and cutting the extra 10 you've added in half, which gives you 15 plus 5.

"Now subtract the original number, 15, and you end up with 5.

"This will work for any number."

"One thing's for certain," said Polly, looking at Mortimer slurp down his dessert. "You don't have to be a mind reader to know that Mortimer loves lime Jell-O!"

The Case of the Lost Package

Wendy White hurried from her classroom as soon as the final bell had rung.

"Where are you headed so fast?" asked her good friend Samantha Scarlet.

"I'm going to meet my dad at work," Wendy replied. "He's on the early shift today, so he gets off about the same time that school lets out. It gives us a chance to ride home together."

Wendy's father was the postmaster of their town. Wendy was proud of him. She thought that the post office was a pretty cool place to work.

"See you tomorrow, Samantha," called Wendy as she ran down the street.

The Clue Club kids live in a small town. The post office could get busy at times, but usually Wendy's dad had a pretty quiet job. Wendy was not prepared for the scene that greeted her as she ran up to the post office.

What in the world is going on here? Wendy wondered.

The post office was surrounded by half-a-dozen police cars — probably every police car in town.

Wendy ran inside. She spotted her dad behind the counter being questioned by the chief of police and his sergeant.

"Dad!" shouted Wendy. "Are you all right?"

"Yes, Wendy, I'm fine," her dad replied.

"Then why are all these officers here?" she asked.

"Well, miss," began the police sergeant, "it seems that a priceless object from ancient Greece was recently stolen from the Hobart Art Museum."

Hobart is a large city not too far from the town.

"Wow!" said Wendy, intrigued by the story. "What was taken?"

"An eight-foot-long javelin, believed to have been used in the ancient Greek Olympics," continued the sergeant. "It really is a priceless object."

"But what does that have to do with my dad?" asked Wendy. "You don't think he had anything to do with the robbery?"

"No, not at all," replied the sergeant, smiling. "We received an anonymous tip. The informant told us that the thief packed up the javelin and took it to this post office today to mail it to his accomplice somewhere else in the United States."

Wendy and Mr. White joined the police in the back of the post office, where the packages were kept. They were searching back there to figure out what type of box could hold an eight-foot-long javelin.

Mr. White pulled out samples of all the different types of boxes that had been dropped off at the post office that day.

"This box is three feet wide by four feet tall," explained Mr. White, holding up an almost square box and showing it to the police. "So there's no way it could have fit in here."

"This one is six feet wide by two feet tall," continued Mr. White, holding up a long thin box. "Again, it's too small.

"And finally," he said, holding up a long bulky box, "the largest box that was dropped off here today is this one, which is seven feet wide by four feet tall. It appears that none of the boxes mailed today are big enough to hold the eight-foot-long javelin."

"Are you certain that these are all the boxes that were mailed today?" asked the chief.

"I'll take another look around," said Mr. White, "just to make doubly sure."

As Mr. White searched around the back of the post office, Wendy looked at the three sample boxes that her dad had just shown to the police. She took a tape measure. Then she held each box in her hands, turning it around, examining it from all angles, and measuring it.

A few minutes later her dad came back to the chief and sighed.

"It's just as I thought, chief," he said. "Those are definitely the only large packages mailed out today."

"Then that tip we got must have been false," said the sergeant. "There's not a box in the whole place that's eight feet long. The longest box here is just seven feet long."

"I guess the tip was a phoney," said the chief. "Okay, guys, let's get out of here and let Mr. White finish up his work."

"Just a minute," said Wendy, who strolled over, tape measure in hand. "I've got a suspect for you, Chief. Mr. Albert Graham of 604 Pine Drive, Franklin Square, New York. Since using the U.S. mail makes this a federal case, maybe the FBI will help you check him out."

"Wait a minute," said the sergeant. "I

didn't see any eight-foot-long boxes."

"I didn't find any eight-foot boxes, either," she explained. "But I found the next best thing. The box that will help catch the thief!"

What did Wendy find?

Solution
The Case of the Lost Package

Wendy pointed to a seven-foot-wide by four-foot-tall box. "It's true that this box is only seven feet wide," began Wendy. "However, if an eight-foot-long javelin was placed *diagonally* across this box, there would be plenty of room."

Mr. White checked his records and, sure enough, the only seven-by-four-foot box brought to the post office that day was the one that Wendy had pointed out — the one addressed to Albert Graham.

The police checked with the FBI, and the FBI confirmed that Albert Graham was a known seller of stolen art objects. Graham was arrested and soon revealed the name of the thief who had planned to send him the package.

The police chief sent a very nice thank-you note to Wendy, offering her a job on the force when she gets out of school!

The Case of the Missing Baseball Cards

Georgie Green hurried down the street.

He was going to the baseball card shop where he spent most of his allowance. Georgie loved to collect baseball cards.

"Hi, Georgie," said the store clerk. "How many packs today?"

"Three, please," said Georgie. He handed over his money, then took the three packs of cards from the clerk.

"Wow!" exclaimed Georgie. "I always love getting new packs. Thanks a lot!"

"Sure thing," said the clerk. "See you next week."

Georgie rushed home and ran straight to his room. He opened his bottom desk drawer. Then he pulled out a locked metal strongbox and placed it on top of the desk.

Just then, his pet monkey, Bingo, came bounding into Georgie's bedroom.

"Hey, Bingo!" said Georgie. "I got three new packs today."

Georgie walked across the room to his closet, with Bingo following closely at his heels. He opened the door and stood on his tippytoes, reaching up to the closet's highest shelf. Georgie stuck his hand under a stack of sweaters and pulled out a key.

He went back to his desk and opened the strongbox with the key. Inside the box were many baseball cards. Georgie smiled. He loved his cards. Just then the doorbell rang.

"Uh-oh," he said. "Someone is early."

The Clue Club was meeting at Georgie's this week. But they weren't supposed to start for another half hour.

Georgie placed the three packs he had just bought into the box, then closed the lid and locked it.

Quickly, Georgie put the box back into

his drawer and went downstairs to answer the door. It was Peter Plum.

"Hi, Peter," said Georgie. "You're early."

"I hope you don't mind," said Peter. "My mom was going out, so she dropped me off."

"Come on in," said Georgie.

"What's that key for?" asked Peter, closing the door behind him.

Georgie had forgotten that he was still holding the key to the strongbox.

"Oh, this," he said, trying to decide whether or not to share his secret with Peter.

"I'm going to show you something, Peter," said Georgie, "but you've got to promise not to tell anyone else."

"Sure, Georgie," replied Peter. "I can keep a secret."

Georgie took Peter up into his room.

Georgie opened his desk drawer and pulled out the strongbox. He opened it with the key and showed Peter what was inside.

"Wow!" said Peter. "You have an amazing collection. You have Nolan Ryan's rookie card! Cool!"

"I don't want anyone else finding out about this, Peter," said Georgie. "It will be our little secret."

"Sure, Georgie," said Peter. "Don't you want to open these?" Peter pointed to the new packs.

"I'll wait till later after the Clue meeting. I don't want everyone grabbing at these." Georgie locked the box and put it in his closet.

The doorbell rang again. The two friends went downstairs.

"Ready to lose?" said Polly Peacock as she walked in. She could never resist teasing her opponents before a game of Clue Jr.

"I'm afraid not, Polly," said Mortimer Mustard, who was on the other team. "Just because you've won three games in a row doesn't mean that you'll win again."

"Anybody up for playing instead of talking about it?" said Georgie as he pulled the Clue Jr. game off the shelf.

The game was set up and Mortimer tossed the die to begin.

When the game was over, six members of the Clue Club got up and pushed their cards away.

"I can't believe you won again, Polly!" said Samantha Scarlet.

Peter, Wendy White, and Samantha stomped off to the kitchen to get drinks.

Georgie went outside to play catch with Polly and Mortimer.

"Can I borrow your baseball glove?" asked Mortimer. "This ball is hurting my hand."

"Sure," said Georgie. "It's up in my room. I'll go get it."

Georgie ran up the stairs to his room. But when he stepped into the room he yelled, "My cards!" His strongbox was sitting out on his desk. It had been opened and several cards were missing.

Georgie ran down the stairs, looking for Peter. He found Peter in the kitchen drinking a glass of juice. He also found a baseball wrapper.

"Thanks a lot, Peter," said Georgie. "I share a secret with you and this is what you do? Where are the cards?" Georgie held the wrapper up to Peter's face.

"What are you talking about, Georgie?" said Peter.

"While I was outside just now, someone went into my room, opened my strongbox, and took some of my baseball cards," Georgie said. "Since you were the only one who knew where the key was, it had to be you."

Just then, a loud pop came from the other room. Polly Peacock looked into the room and said, "Georgie, it wasn't Peter who took your cards. I can tell you who did it!"

Who took the baseball cards?

Solution
The Case of the Missing Baseball Cards

Everyone ran into the other room. There sat Bingo blowing big bubbles with the bubble gum from some of Georgie's baseball cards. The opened packs and cards were sitting on the floor.

"Bingo!" shouted Georgie. "How could you do this?" Then Georgie remembered that Bingo had been in his room when he hid the key and the box.

Georgie rescued as many of the cards as possible and apologized to Peter. He then found a new spot to hide his baseball cards. A spot that even Bingo didn't know about!

"Well, Polly, you won *again*," Mortimer said.

"I know," Polly said. "When it comes to finding clues, I don't monkey around!"

The Case of the Stolen Jewel

Peter Plum opened the cigar box he used to keep his allowance in. He counted out the money, and shoved the bills and change into his pocket. He then grabbed his coat and ran out of the house.

He hurried down the street. He was on a mission.

"Ah, here at last," said Peter. He had arrived at Jules' Jewels, the local jewelry store. His mom had a birthday coming up, and Mr. Jules always gave Peter and his friends special discounts when they bought presents for family members.

Peter had asked Samantha Scarlet and Georgie Green to meet him at the store.

"Hi, Peter," said Samantha, as Peter arrived.

"I love looking around in this place," said Georgie.

"Then let's go in," said Peter, opening the door.

"Good morning, Mr. Jules," said Peter as he entered the store. "I've been saving up my allowance for weeks so that I can buy my mom a nice present."

Peter was so intent on the gift for his mom that he failed to notice at first that Mr. Jules was very upset.

"Mr. Jules, are you all right?" Samantha asked.

"Oh, kids, it's terrible," Mr. Jules replied. "Last week someone robbed my store."

"Oh, no," said Peter. "What was stolen?"

"I had a very large, extremely valuable diamond in the safe," explained Mr. Jules. "Mr. Stoler, the bank president, had bought it for his wife for their wedding anniversary. I was planning on setting the diamond in a ring this week. I was just keeping it in the safe until the ring was ready. And now . . . now it's gone."

"Gee, that's awful," said Peter.

"Yes," replied the jeweler. "And what's even worse is that the police have named Frank, my trusted employee, as the number one suspect!"

"Frank!" exclaimed Georgie. "I can't believe it. He's worked for you for years."

"Five years," said Mr. Jules. "I trusted him with the combination to my safe. He and I are the only two people in the world who know that combination."

"Why do the police think that Frank took the diamond?" asked Peter.

"There was no damage to the safe," explained Mr. Jules. "No signs of it being broken into. So it was obvious that only someone who knew the combination could have taken the jewel. That left Frank and me. *I* certainly didn't take it.

"When the police came they searched us both, but neither had the jewel on us."

"Did the police arrest Frank right away?" asked Peter.

"No," replied Mr. Jules. "I guess they figured I could have taken it and tried to frame Frank. But since he was the prime suspect, the police bugged his phone. They overheard two interesting conversations. In the first, Frank was trying to figure out 'how to sell the stone.' In the other, he was telling his girlfriend he left something special 'in the mouse hole.' "

"Wow!" said Samantha. "It sounds like he is guilty."

"That's what the police thought," said Mr. Jules. "Although Frank says that when he was talking about selling the stone, he was talking about selling some gravel from his cousin's farm. And he said that he has been having trouble with mice in his house, so he put some mouse poison into a mouse hole in his basement. He claims that was what he meant by something special in the mouse hole."

"But the police didn't believe him?" asked Georgie.

"No," said Mr. Jules. "They arrested him a few days ago."

"You know, Mr. Jules," began Peter, "we're pretty good amateur detectives. Would you mind if we looked around a bit?"

"Go ahead," said Mr. Jules. "But the police already searched the store from top to bottom. They found no diamond and no mouse holes, either."

The three friends got to work searching every square inch of the jewelry store.

Samantha took an inventory list of all the items in the store and hovered over a display cabinet, checking the merchandise against the list. Georgie examined one of the wall display cabinets looking for clues. Peter checked behind the display cabinets, where Mr. Jules usually stood.

"Everything here is on the list," Samantha announced. "No extra diamonds."

"I know," said Mr. Jules. "I checked that already."

Next, Peter checked the store's back-room office, where Mr. Jules kept track of his business.

"I've looked through all the drawers and file cabinets," reported Peter. "I even looked in the wastebaskets. No diamond in there, either."

"Like I told you, the police and I have already been through all this."

During his search, Peter saw a personal computer on a stand in a corner.

"Cool computer, Mr. Jules," said Peter. "Do you have any games on it?"

"I honestly don't know," replied Mr. Jules. "Frank was the one who used it. He kept track of sales figures, sent out letters to customers, that type of thing."

"Frank used the computer, huh?" said Peter, rubbing his chin thoughtfully. Then he snapped his fingers and a broad smile spread across his face.

"Mr. Jules!" he announced. "I know where to find your missing diamond!"

Where is the missing diamond?

Solution
The Case of the Stolen Jewel

"As soon as you told me that Frank was the one who used the computer, it came to me," explained Peter. "Frank said that there was something special "in the mouse hole." We all thought at first that he was talking about mice. But I'll bet he meant the computer's mouse." Peter picked up the mouse. "This allows you to point and click on objects on the screen."

Mr. Jules got Peter a screwdriver. Peter unscrewed the bottom of the mouse, and sure enough, there was the diamond.

"Nice work, Peter," said Samantha.

"Yeah," added Georgie. "Way to go."

"I can't thank you enough, Peter," said Mr. Jules.

"It was my pleasure," said Peter. "Now, I still need a birthday gift for my mom."

The police had the evidence needed to convict Frank, and Peter's mom got an extra-special birthday present.